The NORTH CAROLINA
Night Before
Christmas

SWEETWATER
PRESS

The North Carolina Night Before Christmas
Copyright © 2006 by Sweetwater Press
Produced by Cliff Road Books

ISBN-13: 987-1-58173-394-5
ISBN-10: 1-58173-394-1

Printed in Italy

The NORTH CAROLINA Night Before Christmas

E.J. Sullivan

Illustrated by

Ernie Eldredge

SWEETWATER
PRESS

'Twas a North Carolina night before Christmas,
and from Hickory to Hatteras,
Not a creature was fussin'—Mom wasn't
even mad at us.

Our stockings hung
on the porch where
Santa could reach
To fill 'em with NASCAR
toys and stuff for
the beach.

Baby Sister was snuggled all safe in her bed,
With visions of Tar Heels cheers in her head.
And me in my Wolf Pack jammies, and Luke in his Blue Devils,
Were just settling down with our old dog, Rebel.

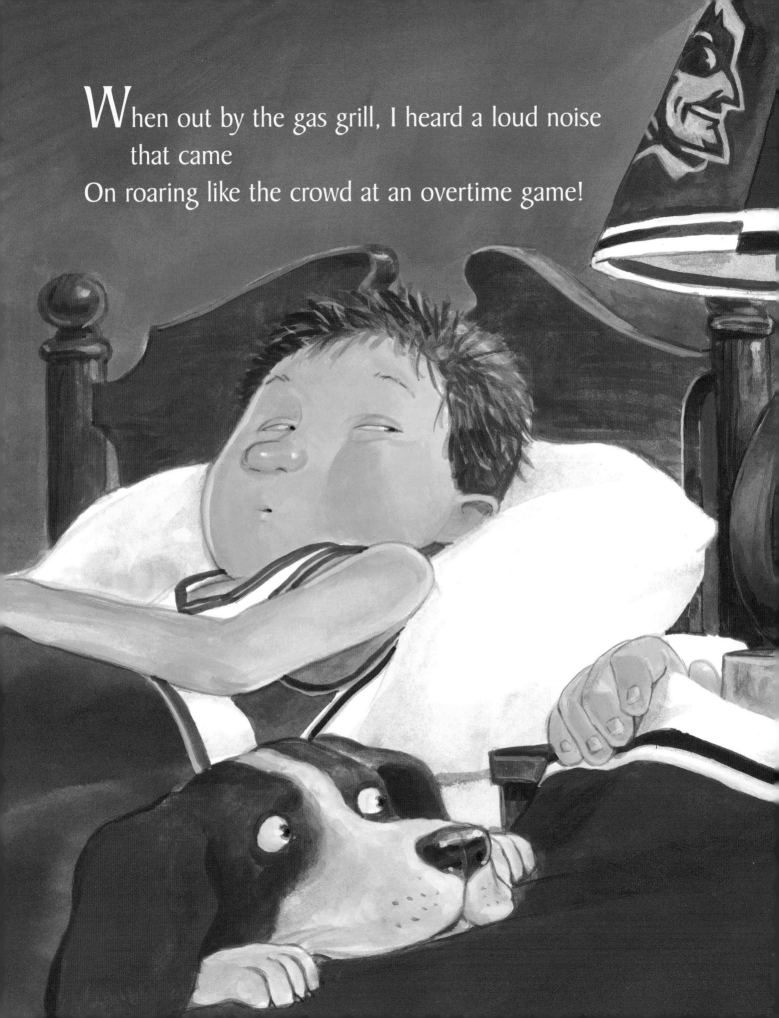

When out by the gas grill, I heard a loud noise that came
On roaring like the crowd at an overtime game!

I sprang to the window and up
went my hackles,
So I armed myself with Dad's
new surf-fishing tackle!

The moon was as bright as the new dollar store
They put in down the road—it's open all hours!
Then what to my wondering eyes should I spy
But a basketball team bus flying on by...

With a li'l ol' driver so lively and
    quick,
He could'a made it 'round Rockingham
    ten times in a lick!

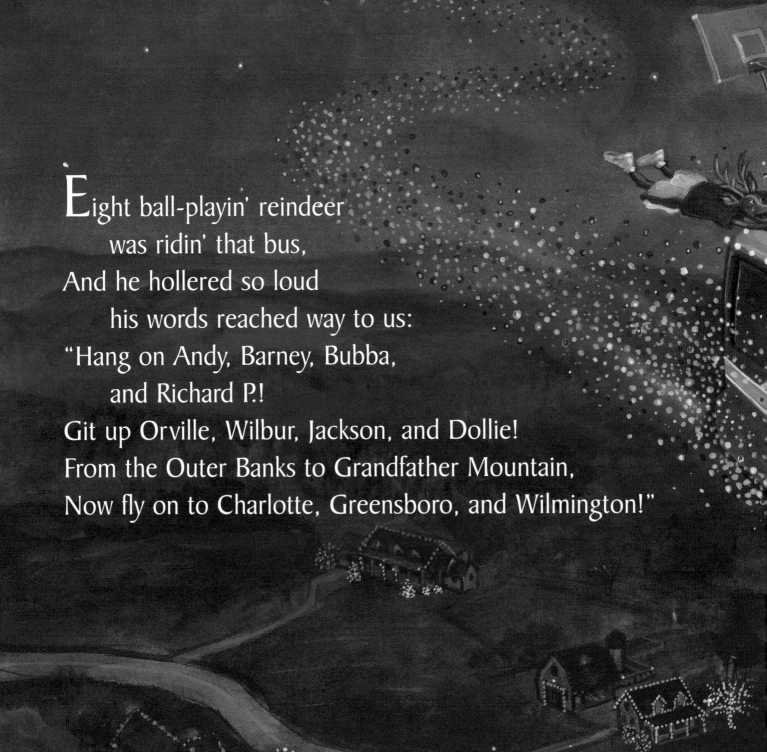

Eight ball-playin' reindeer
        was ridin' that bus,
And he hollered so loud
        his words reached way to us:
"Hang on Andy, Barney, Bubba,
        and Richard P.!
Git up Orville, Wilbur, Jackson, and Dollie!
From the Outer Banks to Grandfather Mountain,
Now fly on to Charlotte, Greensboro, and Wilmington!"

You know when the weathermen come on TV
Showing how hurricanes are gonna blow us all away?
That's how this bus made the sky weird and yellowy.
Got me so worked up I needed a glass of sweet tea!

As I finished my drink, I saw our old pine tree shake
When the bottom of that big bus started to scrape.
I looked up through the limbs and caught him red-handed—
On our Old Baldy birdhouse Santa'd crash landed!

Bless his heart. He looked just like Blackbeard to me,
With his wild hair and beard tangled up in that tree.
Mom's always saying I should help folks who are older,
So I helped him get down on our John Deere mower.

Santa headed inside with a bit of a limp,
And filled all our stockings with boiled peanuts
and shrimp.

Then he looked right at me, and before going out the door
Slapped on top of the TV some new bass fishing lures.

He fired up his bus and soon he
    was gone,
All the while yelling at those deer to
    get on.
But I heard him holler out as his rig
    sped away,
"Merry Christmas, North Carolina,
    I wish I could stay!"